P9-APD-220

FEB 2 6 2020

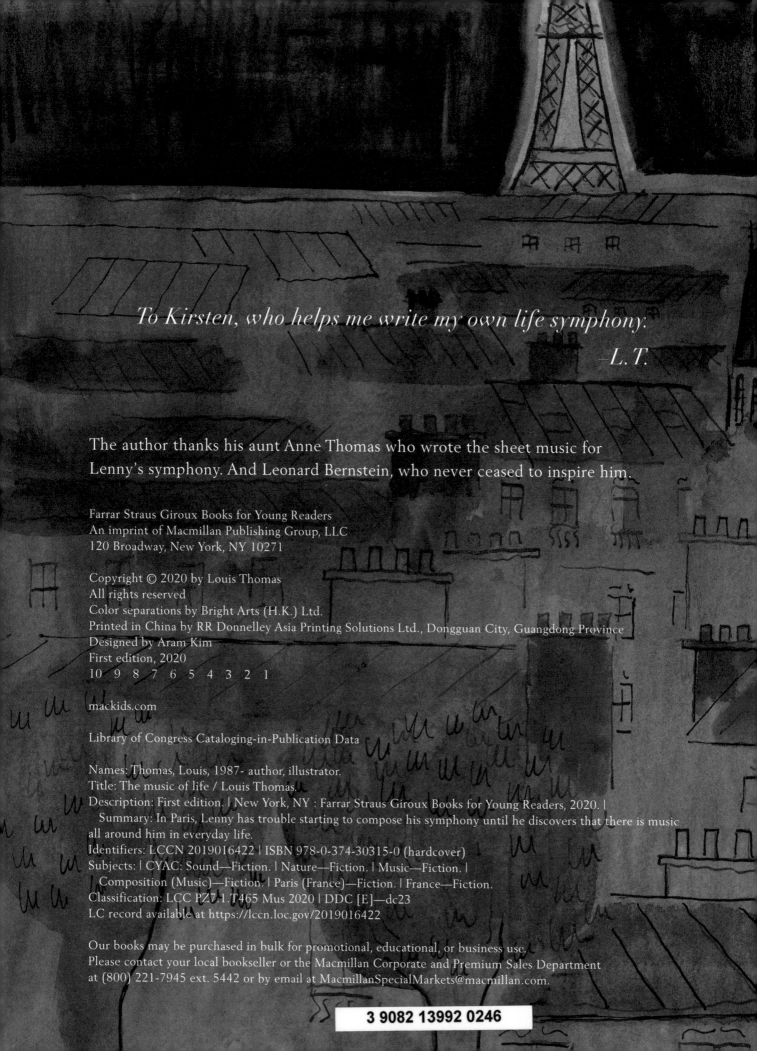

To Kirsten, who helps me write my own life symphony.
—L.T.

The author thanks his aunt Anne Thomas who wrote the sheet music for
Lenny's symphony. And Leonard Bernstein, who never ceased to inspire him.

Farrar Straus Giroux Books for Young Readers
An imprint of Macmillan Publishing Group, LLC
120 Broadway, New York, NY 10271

Copyright © 2020 by Louis Thomas
All rights reserved
Color separations by Bright Arts (H.K.) Ltd.
Printed in China by RR Donnelley Asia Printing Solutions Ltd., Dongguan City, Guangdong Province
Designed by Aram Kim
First edition, 2020
10 9 8 7 6 5 4 3 2 1

mackids.com

Library of Congress Cataloging-in-Publication Data

Names: Thomas, Louis, 1987- author, illustrator.
Title: The music of life / Louis Thomas.
Description: First edition. | New York, NY : Farrar Straus Giroux Books for Young Readers, 2020. |
   Summary: In Paris, Lenny has trouble starting to compose his symphony until he discovers that there is music
all around him in everyday life.
Identifiers: LCCN 2019016422 | ISBN 978-0-374-30315-0 (hardcover)
Subjects: | CYAC: Sound—Fiction. | Nature—Fiction. | Music—Fiction. |
   Composition (Music)—Fiction. | Paris (France)—Fiction. | France—Fiction.
Classification: LCC PZ7.1.T465 Mus 2020 | DDC [E]—dc23
LC record available at https://lccn.loc.gov/2019016422

Our books may be purchased in bulk for promotional, educational, or business use.
Please contact your local bookseller or the Macmillan Corporate and Premium Sales Department
at (800) 221-7945 ext. 5442 or by email at MacmillanSpecialMarkets@macmillan.com.

3 9082 13992 0246

The Music of Life

Louis Thomas

TRENTON VETERANS
MEMORIAL LIBRARY
2790 Westfield
Trenton, MI 48183
(734) 676-9777

Farrar Straus Giroux
New York

*A*t night when everyone else is asleep, you can be sure that an artist—someone, somewhere—is awake. Artists love to create at night.

Lenny is an artist. He's a music composer.

"I'm going to write a symphony tonight!" he said to his cat, Pipo.

But he'd been sitting at his desk for hours, and
not a single note of music had come to mind.

In front of Lenny, there was simply a blank page.

He was starting to feel stuck,

when suddenly . . .

Pipo gave him an idea!

Lick ♪
Lick ♪
Lick

Lenny ran back to his blank page to write it down.

And then . . .

Plic
Ploc
Pluc

"Oho! What is this?"
The leaking sink gave Lenny *another* idea.

"It's not a symphony, but it *feels* like music!"
So he wrote those notes down, too.

Tweet
Tweet
Tweet

And before the sun was even up, Lenny heard birds gathering in the trees.

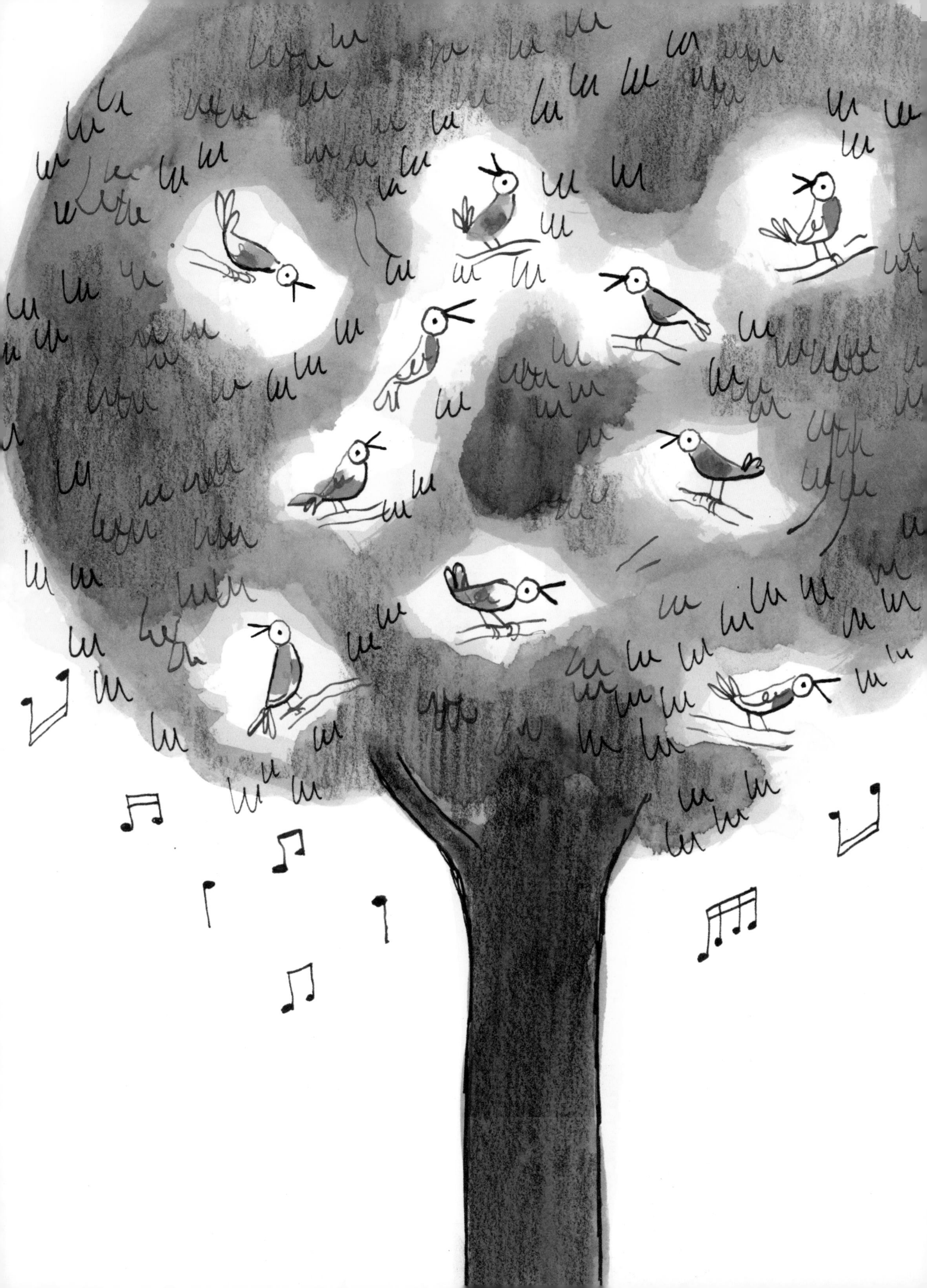

"Do you hear what I hear, Pipo?" Lenny asked his cat.
"More ideas are floating up to my ears!"

Below his window, in the dark streets before dawn, Lenny saw his neighbors begin to stir.

Ms. Doinel was riding by on her bicycle.
The corner baker was rolling up shutters.
And just there, a dog was barking.

Ting
Ting
Ting

Woof
Woof
Woof

"It's not a symphony, but it *feels* like music,"
Lenny told Pipo as he wrote down these notes, too.
That's when . . .

Buzz
Buzz
Buzz

He heard another idea.

"I should go outside!" Lenny said.

"There will be even
more music in the park."

So he ran.

He passed the beehives. Beyond them,

the park was full of sounds, full of notes!

The baby was laughing.

He-he-he
Ho-ho-ho
Hu-hu-hu

The gardener was raking.

Swift
Swift
Swift

The motorcyclist was speeding.

The squirrels were nut-cracking.

Snails were passing by in silence.
Silences are important in a symphony,
thought Lenny.

The pigeons were cooing.

Cooo
Rooo
Cooo
Rooo

The jogger was huffing.

The ducks were quacking.

"Oh yes!" said Lenny. "*Now* this feels like a symphony."

As Lenny walked home later that morning, he looked down at his paper. It wasn't blank at all.

It was full of notes. Full of ideas.
Full of *life*.